SQUARE HEART

WHEN WORDS JUST AREN'T ENOUGH

Square Heart
by Steve Stinson

ISBN-979-8-9900137-1-1

A Stinson Art Studio publication.
Cover art by: Steve Stinson
Copyright 2023 Steve Stinson

Printed in the United States of America Worldwide Electronic &
Digital Rights Worldwide English Language Print Rights

For the B-girl

Square Heart is a story told entirely in pictures, sort of a silent movie in print.

It is for anyone who has tried on more than one heart, only to keep looking. I think of it as a long-form Valentine.

The
Beginning